Ca

a novella series

By S.W. CANNON

Casey Canyon's dishonest choices lead him to huge trouble in his love life and possibly in his career. A destructive love triangle and near misses with the law, leave this police officer in a complicated dilemma. Will he choose Sam or Meredith, the law or crime? The decisions may have already been made for him.

Stay tuned for the rest of the Canyon series:
Canyon Deep and Canyon Echo.

CASEY CANYON

Nonnac Content & Press

Nonnac Content & Press
Birmingham, Alabama

This is a work of fiction. All of the characters, places, incidents, dialogue and events portrayed in this novella are either products of the author's imagination or are used fictitiously and NOT to be construed as real. Any resemblance to actual events or locales or persons, living or dead, is entirely coincidental.

For information AuthorS.W.Cannon@gmail.com
www.AuthorSWCannon.com

ISBN- 978-0-9895183-0-7

Library of Congress Control Number: 2013946704

1. Fiction 2. Suspense 3. Thriller 4. Crime 5. Urban Fiction

Cover Design by S. W. Cannon and Ronald Crawford, Jr.

Dedications

I dedicate this book to
my sons Rick, Nathan and Justin
my Goddaughter Jasmine (Rod) Grizzard
my Godgranddaughter Eden Grizzard

**my inspiration and the love of my life,
Christopher Cannon**

my copy editing guru Shelia Bryant

and

the peanut gallery of beta readers who helped me perfect my plot: Sheena Agyare, Lionel Beckles, Jabre' Bell, Elizabeth Brown, Veronica Carmichael, Lori Hornsby, Carla Menefee-Lewis, Pasocca Merritt, Djuana Smith, and, LaVonda Willoughby.

Acknowledgements

Without the support of family, you can get little achieved in life. A special thank you to my family: Wertna G. Story, Lutisha Story-Jackson, Ronald Jackson, Micah Brittingham-Jackson, Toshiba Story-Williams, Elijah Williams, Sandra Dodd, Robert Dodd, David Ware, Jr., Ashunii Thomas, Erica Lamarr, Arthur Latham, Jr., Clea Latham Lacey, LaSalle Latham, Christopher Story, Devon Story, Graylen Pruitt, Olympia Story-Oliver, Meca Story-Jackson, Detrick Story, Graylen Story, Jr., Yoshida Story, Damion Story, Kendra Story, Curtis Coleman, Jr., Pekeisha Bennett-Jones, Alan Hazelrig, II, Debra Hazelrig and last but certainly not least, my sisters-in-books ITC12 Book Club of Birmingham, Alabama. If I have left anyone out, please charge it to my mind and not my heart.

I-65 S

"Stop sounding pitiful. You know you are just greedy like the rest of these men out here..." - Candy

It seemed like only moments after I pushed her out of the moving SUV that I confirmed hearing the sound of sirens coming toward us on the freeway. No time to hash it out. No time to fix it. Evidently she's okay because she's still screaming obscenities my way. Upon jumping out of the patrol car, the officers quickly demand I place my hands on the vehicle.

"*He pushed me out of the truck while it was moving!*" Samantha yells, with her Puerto Rican accent.

"*Tell them why Sam. Tell them you were fighting me while I was driving. I could have killed us both.*" I say.

"*I didn't touch you!!*" Samantha exclaims.

The officers separate us to get our individual stories of what happened. I know it will be hard for these podunk, small town police officers to believe my six foot, 230 pound ass was not as aggressive as this five foot, three inch woman. Lord only knows if I'd identified myself as a fellow police officer whether it would have helped or hurt me. Luckily for me, in her full speed Spanglish, she couldn't keep her story straight. Even these good ole country boys can respect my ever vigilant account of the events that led to her rolling downhill in the grass alongside Interstate 65. After running my name from the driver's license I gave them, they were satisfied enough. It was a close call they didn't see the Fraternal Order of Police card sitting in my wallet parallel to the space I pulled my license from; it also read Casey Canyon.

I take a deep breath as they drive away with her cuffed and crying in the backseat. I look from the police car growing smaller in the distance to the card in my hands with the incident report number scribbled across the front. I then look to her Altima, headlights still on and doors still flung wide open. I knew about that hot Puerto Rican temper before I decided to be with her. Tonight's events make it hard to remember she really is a good person in addition to being fine as hell. Despite her heritage-induced, anger management problem, I can't leave her in jail.

With dread in my voice, I call her sister to arrange for her bond.

It's the next afternoon, I don't want to get up but I manage to do so. The shower did little to awaken my senses but little could after such a rough night. As I shine my badge then carefully pin it over the left pocket of my uniform shirt, it is hard to believe I came so close to losing my job just last night. Domestic violence is grounds for automatic termination in our police department. My mom is an ex-cop and so is my uncle, who happens to be my father figure. I couldn't bare their disappointment. I've already done some things that left a bad taste in a few of my superiors' mouths. I love my job but I know that is the reason I am still a beat cop. I am good at what I do in the scheme of things. I am an even better Field Training Officer. I teach rookies what they should do, not what I do. I will admit I take liberties with my interpretation of the rules but they don't know half the stuff I do.

When I power my phone back on, multiple notifications from the heap of text messages and voicemails from Sam send my cell hopping across the bed. Well at least she made it home. You would think after my experiences with difficult women in the past that I would beware of dramatic, violent girlfriends.

It's harder when your feelings are stronger; when you think if you just put up with it you'll be with who you want to be with. I mean I've wanted her since I first saw her brown skin show from an off the shoulder dress that clung to her perfect shape. I have an affinity for a nice hip span and an ample ass but rarely is it coupled with the intelligence Sam possesses and sometimes hides with her anger driven decisions.

"*Heeeeeey baby. What you doing?*" I croon.

"*Hey babe, I am trying not to get sick from this crazy Alabama weather. It was just in the 70's yesterday and overnight I need a scarf on to protect myself from the cold. Did you miss me last night?*" the female voice says.

"*I always do. I had to work extra last night but I will be there tonight to make it up to you. Okay?*" I say with a slight smile.

"*Sounds great, I'll see you then.*" she replies before hanging up.

I need this shift to go by smoothly. Tonight I need the calmness that Meredith brings. Just as she is opposite in height than Sam, standing at six feet tall, her personality is opposite too. Meredith isn't easily riled. She reminds me of myself, more nonchalant than not. The only time I get peace from Sam is when she goes back home to visit family in Puerto Rico. I can't explain why I'm stuck between the two of them except to say both of them have qualities that make up my perfect woman. It is not a love triangle void of pain for me. I really love them both and can't choose between them.

Riding down Carraway Boulevard, I have to turn the heat on in the patrol car. Meredith is right, it is cold. Although I'm not sure if I would say it's Alabama weather. It is definitely Birmingham weather. Looking up from the climate controls, I realize a moment slower and I'd have missed the tinted out Caprice run the stop sign. I hit my lights and siren. The hesitation of the car to pull over made it seem as though the driver may have thought better of making a run for it. Smart move for them to stop and cut the engine, I am in a police brutality kind of mood today. Lack of sleep and this girl still calling my phone leaving angry messages has heightened my irritability. I cannot see through the dark tint spread across the back window, so I unsnap the holster to my gun and leave my hand hovering over the grip. As I approach the driver window, the smell of marijuana is potent. I ask the driver to step out of the car and place his hands on the hood of the car. Gun drawn, I check the inside of the car for anyone else that may be present. The car is now empty.

"*Mr. Officer, I wasn't speeding.*" says the teenager.

"*No, you were going rather slowly when you went right through that stop sign*" I retort. "*Do you have any drugs or weapons on you or in the car?*"

"*No sir.*" he replies.

"*Do you mind if I check your vehicle?*" I said sternly as I patted him down, emptying his pockets onto the hood of the car.

"*This isn't my car. I don't know what's in it.*" he says, voice trembling.

Likely story you lil rapper wannabe. With enough probable cause from his air freshener of choice, I cuff him and sit him in the backseat of the patrol car before searching his vehicle. Going straight for the hiding place of choice for most in a hurry to hide something, I pull a gallon sized Ziploc bag from under the driver seat. Look-a-here, enough for a distribution charge. I go to the back of my squad car with a huge smile on my face. This arrest will top off my monthly numbers nicely. I usually do more sleeping on this 3pm to 11pm shift than arresting. Already in tears, my newest apprehension pushes his words of explanation out of his mouth.

"*Mannnnnn my momma gonna kill me. I swear it isn't mine officer. I just enrolled in school at Lawson State and everything. Please don't arrest me. My momma won't even have the money to bail me out.*" he says.

"*Oh YOU just enrolled in school, huh? Boy you must think I'm a fool. Okay, I tell you what, where is your college ID?*" I ask in disbelief.

"*It's in the wallet you took from my front pocket. I just got it. It has my picture on it and everything.*" he whines.

I get the wallet off the hood of the patrol car. Erik Parsons, freshman at Lawson State Community College. Date of issuance stated as October, 3, 2011, supporting his story of receiving it a few days ago.

"*I guess you weren't lying about that part of your story. I am going to run the tag on this car. If this car comes back in someone else's name, then I will be inclined to believe your entire story.*" I say with doubt in my voice.

Sure enough the car is registered to a Carlos Parsons. I know that name. That little punk hasn't been anything but trouble around this neighborhood since he was in middle school. This must be his younger brother. I guess their mother finally had a not so bad apple.

"*Is Carlos your brother?*" I interrogate.

"*Yes, sir.*" he says as he hangs his head. "*I usually don't drive any of his cars but I needed to go to the store. I missed the stop sign trying to hurry and get back home.*"

I open the car door. "*Stand up.*" I order. I un-cuff the boy and send him on his way, throwing the weed in my glove compartment. I've always seen drugs as a victimless crime. Not many people are forced onto drugs, just as johns aren't forced to pay prostitutes.

After getting off work, showering and changing clothes, I make a stop before going to Meredith's place. My sister works at a strip club and I promised her I would stop by sometime soon. I call her phone hoping she will be in the dressing room to hear it. This particular club is always under scrutiny from the city council so it will be great if I don't have to go inside.

Luckily she answers, "*Hey Brother. Where you at?*"

"*I am outside. Come out for a minute and bring your purse.*" I respond.

It only took a few minutes for her to sashay out with her big purse on her shoulders and a huge smile on her face. She knows exactly why I made the request.

"*You got a surprise for me?*" she beams.

I pull out the weed I confiscated earlier and pass it to her.

"*Dam. Somebody going be short on a flip but all's fair in love and Mary Jane.*" she celebrates.

"*I am glad you are happy baby girl. I can't stay, Meredith is expecting me.*" I explain as I put the car in gear.

"*You really need to decide who you want to be with because with them knowing about each other, that's a fight waiting to happen. Hell I hope I'm there to see it.*" she says laughing.

"*Do not wish no shit like that on me, Sis. You know I feel bad enough. They don't know I'm still dating both of them but I know I will have to decide* between them. It can't go on like this much longer." I say.

"Stop sounding pitiful. You know you are just greedy like the rest of these men out here. Let me go, my set starts soon. Thanks Bro!" she says happily as she bounces out of the car.

I almost told her that with what happened last night, it should have made my choice easier. But Candy already favors Meredith. She also would definitely have a death match with Sam the next time she saw her if I gave her the details from last night. I could be with Meredith and be alright but I just wonder if alright is good enough. With my track record, Sam and I will be back together in a week but for tonight Meredith will be more than enough.

Using my key I try to quietly come in and maneuver through the house. By the time I reach her bedroom, I see the tv shower her bare back with light. She is asleep, naked and on her stomach. Whew! That is just one of the things I love about this woman. She ALWAYS sleeps naked and right now, she is lying in my favorite position. I quickly but smoothly take my clothes off to join her in the king sized bed. I slide under the covers just as she shifts her weight.

"Babe, I'm glad you finally made it." Meredith whispers

"Yeah, looks like I made it just in time." I whisper back.

I scoot closer up behind her as she turns to her side. I'm not hungry but this spoon is great, I think to myself. My body cups behind hers, I wrap my arms around her and envelope her breasts with my hand as I kiss her back. Gliding a hand down from her breast to between her thighs, I see she has been having good dreams. That erotic triangle is moist and ready. I slowly guide my hardness pass the gap between her butt cheeks into her wetness. As she lets out a slight moan, I match it with more bass. I swear she feels just right every time I enter her. I don't put anything past her but I would attest this thang is shaped just to fit me. This was worth the wait after a long day.

"Babe, my brother was at the club the other night and said he didn't see you working." Meredith says half-jokingly, half-accusingly.

"What are you talking about?" I say using the universal   I-need-more-time-for-a-better-answer reply. I guess the after sex high is over.

"*We didn't go out the other night because you said you had to work at the club. My brother was at the club and said he saw Jordan working but not you.*" she says with her eyes squinting and scanning my face.

"*Jordan was on duty with the city, not the club. He just stopped by there. I was working the club. And who is your brother anyway?*" I say, trying to change the subject.

"*Aasim is just as much my brother as Candy is your sister. We have a bond despite not being blood just like you two. Stop acting like you don't know that. Anyway, I want you to make it up to me tomorrow night.*" she says.

I was just happy we moved on, "*I can do that.*"

Karaoke Anyone?

"Shaking my head, I think to myself obviously God has a sense of humor, as well as swift wrath." - Casey

I had to work the club tonight after my shift and this time I will really be there. I have been coming to this particular strip club since I was 19 years old. Sad to say but it is home, my own Cheers. It was called Magic City II back then, but it's now under new ownership with a new name. After my rookie year with the department, I jumped at the chance to work here. That was 8 years ago. I just hope I don't have to fight one of these young hustlers in here tonight. I am going to let the non-police security officers foot most of the work load tonight. No sooner do I say that than one of them leaves their post as a small crew pays admission at the front door. Now I'm forced to check IDs and do pat downs. As I am patting down the third guy, I feel a bulge in the front pocket of his oversized jeans. I pull a bag out of his pocket and see it is pills cling wrapped tight together.

"*Now why are you trying to bring these in the club. Let me guess, no prescription?*" I accuse.

"*Hey man, Chubb knows I have them on me. Just go get Chubb and tell him Buddha is here.*" he replies.

"*I'm not going to get nobody. You're about to go to jail.*" I command.

Just as I roughly spin his face toward the wall to cuff him, one of his crew walks up with Chubb.

"*He's straight Casey, you can let him in.*" says Chubb

Chubb is the club owner and he usually lets a group of guys he okays to hustle in the club. I guess this Buddha dude is in the new crew. As I let the pressure off of his neck, he spins back around then turns his top lip up and sneers to Chubb "*Your guard dog a little over zealous ain't he?*" As he walks away, I realize I still have his driver's license in my hand. I look at the picture then the name: Aasim Langston, Jr. Where have I heard that name recently? I can't remember but I will remember his face and when I see Mr. Langston on the street, it will be a different story.

Only three days and Sam and I were back hot and heavy. That is the cycle with us. It did not take long after I finally answered the phone for her to claim she needed something done at her house. When I arrived expecting to do a quick repair, she knew just what to wear...just what to do. Afterwards we discussed what happened, as always she explained how sorry she was and as always I forgave her. We made plans for the next night. I already promised Meredith tonight and I knew she was looking forward to it. I knew she deserved it. When I called Meredith she complained of a hard day and opted for a night in. That sounded good to me anyway. I knew Sam was going out with her girlfriends and staying in with Meredith meant I did not have to stay on my toes for once.

As we usually do, Meredith and I had a good night. The next day brought about an unplanned daytime movie date to take the place of last night's decision to stay in. She has dinner plans with friends so I won't have to worry about pulling away to meet Sam later. Meredith and I enjoyed the movie and walked around the mall. I think we really seem to be getting even closer. Sam and her temper are going to end up getting me fired or worse, put in jail. Maybe I can make it work with Meredith. Well that is what I say until I see *her*. It is easy to be strong when I am not in Sam's presence but as soon as I see her and as soon as I hear those r's roll with that accent, I know I am not going anywhere. With Meredith on the other side of town eating with friends, Sam and I attend a birthday gathering for her tia at a karaoke bar. To look at us hugged up, you would never know we had to be in court soon for what happened days ago. The bar was packed; my turn to sing the song I signed up to lip sync seemed to take forever to come up. But as we sit surrounded by her familia, Sam and I just enjoy the drinks and other performances.

I turn toward the bar only to recognize someone within the group of people. She is the friend Meredith met for dinner. I'm sure Meredith is not here because she made no mention of karaoke. In fact not only did she say she was going home after the dinner, but she has never made mention of attending any karaoke bars before. Just as I feel assured, I hear a familiar laugh. I turn and look right in Meredith's face. Jesus, what to do?! I want to move my arm from around Sam. I want to not feel overcome with guilt. I want to be invisible. My chest is pounding hard through my shirt but as time passes, nothing happens. Sam does not see Meredith and although Meredith sees us, she doesn't come over and confront us. I can always count on Meredith not to make a scene but I'll never hear the end of this later. Right when I start to relax, Sam spots Meredith. Jesus, Mary and Joseph! Sam acts out, standing and raising her voice spitting hot Spanish at my face. Finally she gets up and walks out of the bar. I feverishly text message her to come back into the bar as her family looks on. After some coaxing that I am certain was not enough to work, Sam returns to the inside the club. She sits in her chair beside me and commences to put on a show of fake happiness that I'm sure is for Meredith's benefit. Just when you think things could not get any worse, my name is called to sing my song. Vengeance is mine said the Lord. As if I did not feel guilty enough, now I have to go up here on this stage and sing a Keith Sweat song. Shaking my head, I think to myself obviously God has a sense of humor, as well as swift wrath. If I don't sing the song, Sam is going to act a huge fool in this tight ass bar. If I do sing the song, I know it will just hurt Meredith more. I feel I have no choice. I cannot afford for the police to be called, so I take the stage. I try to keep my eyes on the table where I was seated, not necessarily on Sam but in that direction to keep from getting a glimpse of the hurt in Meredith's eyes. I am willing to testify in court that they looped the song due to how long it feels I have been under this spotlight but finally it is over. I go back to my seat and Sam continues her acting. She stands by my chair and dances then takes a seat and begins to be touchy, feely. I am not sure if she is trying to convince Meredith of happily ever after between us or if she is trying to convince herself. Then it happens, as part of the lyrics to a song, Sam sings out "like that bitch Meredith" as she points toward where Meredith is sitting. What the hell? Confident that Meredith couldn't hear her over the music; I lean my head back and cover my face with my hand as I shake my head knowing that Sam will only get worse as time progresses. As I lean my head forward and uncover my face, I feel a tap on my shoulder.

"*May I speak with you outside?*" I hear Meredith's voice say. Are you serious? Did she get up and come over here? I get up and walk away and as I do Sam stands to confront Meredith. If the situation were not serious, their difference in height would be comical. All I can think is "I am NOT in this because it is about to go way too far." When I turn back toward them, blows have already been passed. Meredith and Sam were fighting. Meredith's friends were mingled in and matched up with Sam's family to keep anyone else from jumping in the fight against Meredith. I scoop Sam up and take her outside as Meredith is pulled back by someone in her group. This night couldn't have ended any worse. Sam drove, so she goes to her vehicle when I release her from my grip. I am so mad I don't know who to blame. I elect to walk home. As I walk, I get a call from Meredith. I instantly blame her. If she had not walked over there, this wouldn't have ever happened. Her reaction to my blame let me know that on top of the hurt I'd already supplied her with; the blame was probably a death blow. This can't be life.

A few days have passed and I haven't heard from Meredith. If I know her as I feel I do, she's done with me. I don't want to be bothered with anyone. I don't want to talk. I just have to think about life. This is not what I ever wanted to happen. I guess everything happens for a reason. The three become two and the choice is made. I make the announcement on Facebook that I am going to marry Sam.

Face Off

"I don't trust you. But I trust my sister." - Buddha

You would think that all my family, friends and co-workers that always had something to say about me being with both Meredith and Sam at the same time would have been happy to see a decision was finally made. Those that didn't know about Sam and Meredith saw enough of me with various side chicks to complain that I needed to settle down. Here I am, settling down. I mean I even asked her father for her hand in marriage. I have taken steps to be closer to her family. I plan to make this work. I have even cut off the side females, female associates and female friends. I belong to Sam now.

It did not take long for me to see my vast efforts were not appreciated. Sam and I mainly argued about Meredith in the past. Now we argue about anything, everything. Nothing is ever good enough or nothing is ever the way Sam thinks it should be; her version of perfect. We could not agree on simple things: whether it was how the bills should be paid, when they should be paid, whose house we should live in, when to have children, etc… I found myself wondering if I had made a mistake. I found myself missing Meredith.

I do not know how they came up with the phrase catch 22 nor the words dilemma or conundrum. What I do know is that I seem to be suffering from them all like a disease. I thought it was hard to choose between them before, now I feel I cannot survive with one without the other. One is my ying and the other is my yang. One a fiery volcano and the other a calming ocean, I needed them both to feel balanced. Selfish I know but I do want my cake and eat it too. I've always thought the saying was stupid. Why have cake if you can't eat it? At this point, I have made a commitment. I have finally chosen and I want to try as hard as I can to make it work. But I knew it will never work without Meredith in my life. We were friends before we were ever lovers. I know now, I need her.

Day in and day out, arguing about this and arguing about that with Sam. Today will be the day I reach out to Meredith. When we don't see eye-to-eye, verbal communication does not work for us. An email will be the best way to start things off.

After looking at the empty body of my email for a while, I finally come up with something: "I really want to talk to you and tell you how bad I feel about what happened and as we both know the best way to express ourselves is by writing. That Saturday when I saw you in the back of that club…" At least this is a start. I know I have to acknowledge what happened two weeks ago and I know I have to apologize. The rest was just babbling, I mean what could I say? "I need you like I need air?" Besides the fight, I am sure she has heard by now that I'm getting married. At this point, she wouldn't care if I choked to death.

I waited one day and no response. This is killing me. I didn't realize how much I thought about her until now. There is a special on cell phones today. I usually purchase her cell phone upgrades. I know she would like the one I bought today. I guess I can at least pass on the information. Once again I open my Gmail account but this time I have convinced myself it is just to be a good Samaritan. I begin typing: "FYI. T-Mobile has the G2 phone for free with an upgrade. Only an 18 dollar upgrade fee." After I hit send, I can only think about what a dumb ass she will think I am. I am just going to stop trying to contact her if she doesn't respond this time.

Everything is so undesirably routine: I work, I keep trying at the impossible task of pleasing Sam and I sleep. Each day it repeats itself, an unhappy circle of life. I don't sleep well so the only solitude I really get is in my patrol car. Is it really solitude when all you can do is think about someone who has probably given up on thinking about you? She didn't respond to my second email either. Who would blame her? Right when I get the urge to take my cell from the patrol car's passenger seat to dial her number, a call comes over the police radio.

"*ALL UNITS, WE HAVE A 10-9-100 AT THE TWENTY-THREE HUNDRED BLOCK OF TWELFTH AVENUE NORTH. THAT'S THE TWENTY-THREE HUNDRED BLOCK OF TWELFTH AVENUE NORTH. SUSPECT IS ARMED AND DANGEROUS. HE IS A BLACK MALE, ABOUT 20 YEARS OLD, WEARING BIG BAGGY JEANS, A WHITE T-SHIRT AND A RED HOODIE, LAST SEEN HEADING NORTHWEST TOWARD BARKER PARK.*" says the dispatcher with an excited voice.

That is car 124's beat on the north side near Druid Hills, I am not that far. I hit the lights and sirens as well as the accelerator. On the way, I hear radio chatter about a second suspect. This suspect is running southwest away from Barker Park along Shuttlesworth Drive. If I come up 19th Street North I may run into him around 11th Avenue North. I bear down on the gas with more weight from the urgency of my plan to cut him off. This suspect was a black male, bald, wearing khaki pants, a black polo and about 30 years of age, also armed. Unlike the other suspect, he had sense enough not to commit a crime in an easily recognizable color such as red.

As I come up on 11th Avenue North, I see a dark figure crossing the street toward Oak Hill Cemetery. The first thing that comes into focus is the khaki colored pants and the second thing I see is a bald head. Sure enough as I neared, the black polo is illuminated by my headlights. The suspect picks up speed and runs into the cemetery. Having less than 1000 feet to call in my location, I do so then fling the car door open and put the car in park all in the same motion. If I jump the wrought iron fence closest to the street rather than going up to the entrance, then I'll have a better chance at catching him. I can't let him cross the cemetery and make it to 17th Street. I wasn't a track star in college to allow the officers that would probably be waiting there get him before I do.

Oak Hill has a lot of trees, if it weren't a cemetery it would be scenic enough to be a park in its own right. Filled mostly with head stones, there were still some good sized mausoleums that would make for great cover. With my gun drawn and my ears open, my eyes used the moonlight as an ally. I don't see anyone and right now I can't hear anything but my heart, just then my radio sounds out. The sound scares not only me but apparently the suspect too. He rustles the dry leaves on the ground and drops a bag in my line of sight, giving his position away just behind the tree I was about to walk near.

In a swift motion, we are face to face. Each of our guns were muzzle to forehead on the other. Talk about a face off. I try to regulate my breathing to give a more confident appearance but as soon as my mind replayed the flash of silver that went from down by his hip to up toward my head, my heart dropped. There is no mistaking a SP101 revolver chambered for the .22 long rifle and re-engineered to house eight rounds instead of the traditional six. This Ruger just made distribution. How the fuck does he have one already? I only recognize it because it's been the talk of the department for a few months now. I've seen pictures of this gun positioned at every angle. Those pictures didn't do it justice; this gun is huge! My thoughts that seem to have taken up minutes, are only taking up a few seconds in real time.

"*It's a good day to die.*" the suspect says but not sounding too sure.

"*You don't have to if you drop the gun now.*" I say as my eyes stayed trained on his.

"*I guess Chubb ain't here to settle this one.*" he says.

Immediately my vision pans out from focusing on his eyes to capture his entire face.

"*I knew I would run into you on these streets and you right, Chubb is not here to give you a pass.*" I say, keeping a stern face.

Aasim Langston, Jr. aka Buddha, I still had his license somewhere in a drawer. We don't have real beef aside from his little disrespectful comment at the club, but the situation was in neither of our favor right now.

"*So now what Casey.*" he says, keeping his voice calm.

"*Oh we friends now? Somebody tell you my name and you use it like you know me?*" I say not able to stop my agitation from leaking into my tone.

He gives a half smile before saying, "*Meredith Jones told me your name.*"

What the hell is going on? How does he know Meredith?

"*You don't look like her type.*" I say, raising my top lip a bit in the left corner and holding my gun a little tighter.

"*Don't use a jealous rage as an excuse to shoot me. She'll never forgive you if her brother can't have an open casket funeral.*" he says jokingly but absent the smile.

"*Brother?*" I say out loud but it echoed in my head.

Just as I was about to lose focus into a sea of thought to try and explain his statement, my ears tune in to hear him say, "*Look, it isn't my intention to be a threat to you now that I see your face and know who you are but I can't put this gun down, until I know you won't shoot me. My knowing who you are to my sister doesn't equal you knowing who I am to her.*"

'Aasim is just as much my brother as Candy is your sister....' this statement rings in my ears except it is in Meredith's voice. Why had I not put two and two together before now?

My attention goes from inside my head, to the police lights in the distance in front of me, to the sound of numerous people approaching in the distance from behind me, then back to Aasim. I say *"You want me to trust you but right now you have to trust me first and we don't have much time. Drop your weapon."*

I don't know what he was thinking but I can see police lights swirling on the lens of his eyes and I am sure he realizes as I do, the people approaching from behind me were cops. Aasim looks at me and says, *"I don't trust you. But I trust my sister."* He lowers the gun while keeping his eyes on me. I trust his sister too, obviously with my life.

"Don't put it on the ground. Put it in your waistband under your shirt." I say.

He looks confused but quickly obeys.

"Go north; they are coming in from the west and the east." I instruct.

Aasim turns on his heels to run but before he could take his second step, I say *"Aren't you forgetting something?"* as I point to the ground to the spot where he dropped the bag when my radio startled him. No doubt the bag contains pills, his product of choice. It would be my final show of trust tonight. After looking from me to the ground, he picks up the bag mid-stride as he sprints into the darkness.

I don't pay attention to Sam complaining about the dishes I left in the sink. My mind was still on last night, still trying to grasp what happened. This Buddha dude was Meredith's so-called brother. She spoke about him with such reverence and love, who would have thought he was just a street thug. I cannot even recall the details of any stories she told me involving him but I never would have guessed it would be someone like him.

"*Just because you can't keep your house clean, doesn't mean you can come over here making it harder for me to keep my house clean. Here.*" Sam says, as she hands me my phone.

For the three weeks Sam and I have been engaged, I have had a new cell number that only my job and my family has access to now. I also keep my phone face up on her computer desk without a lock on it when I'm at her place; all of this just to gain her trust and prove I'm doing right this time, all to please Miss Unappeasable. I look down at the phone and I have one email notification. I open my email and my pulse begins to pump faster in my neck, it is from

Meredith. As if Sam could see what I see, I immediately turn my phone over on my lap. I'm surprised she didn't look at it. I guess three weeks of no suspicious activity on my phone nor from me inspired her give up checking after me.

"Hey I'm sorry I left the dishes in the sink. But I did notice this morning the trash was getting full. I'll take it outside on my way to the car. I left a few things at my house that I will need tonight. I am going to go ahead and leave so I won't be late trying to stop by and get them. I will call you later." I say, trying not to push the words out of my mouth too quickly.

I resist the urge to read the email as soon as I get in the car. I drive down the block and pull into the gas station. I try to convince myself that I wanted a Cherry Coke anyway, but I had barely put the car in park before I was reaching for my cell phone.

'My brother told me what you did. I just wanted you to know I really appreciate it. You could have arrested him just to get back at me. Even though I know you well enough to know you wouldn't do that, you still went above and beyond given the circumstances. Thank you again.' The message is short but sweet and just the crack I need to try to wedge the door open wider.

I quickly reply, hoping my words don't give away my excitement. I want them to give the impression that everything is alright but in reality those five little sentences she sent made my heart sing. It is as close as I've gotten to her in weeks. If I was not certain before it is confirmed now, I miss her.

"*It was no problem. I know how you feel about your family, so I will never let anything happen to them if I can help it. How have you been?*" I try to keep my reply short too. I also want to create an opportunity for the email to go from a thank you/you're welcome to an actual conversation.

After ten minutes of waiting on a reply, I put the phone down and drive out of the gas station parking lot. I went from hopeful to doubtful in those ten minutes. She probably has no intention of sending another email. After all, she has already said thank you. What else would she have to say to me?

Roll call is a blur. I pay attention just in time to hear the lieutenant give a familiar description. A black male, about 5 feet, 11 inches tall and 230 pounds, bald head, mustache with full beard to side burns and brown skin tone. Apparently someone saw Buddha close enough to give a pretty good description but not good enough to exclude a large segment of black males thanks to an appearance made popular by rapper Rick Ross. For now, no one would be looking for Buddha.

I check my email repeatedly during my shift to no avail. My fear bubbles in my throat. Maybe she has moved on as I've tried to in just three short weeks. Maybe she is with someone else and she is happy. After all, I did have my chance. If I have lost her, then I have nothing else to lose. I succeed in dialing her number without interruption from the police dispatcher this time. The phone rings and on the third ring:

"*Hello.*" Meredith says.

"*I need you.*" I respond.

Quid Pro Quo

"It's my opinion that you lie to yourself wayyyyy more than you lie to me." - Meredith

She probably only answered because she didn't recognize the number. But she had to recognize my voice. I don't know if she knows I can't take it if she rejects me right now or if God himself is whispering in her ear asking her to be kind, however Meredith surprisingly continues the conversation.

"*I don't think you need me anymore Casey. You made your choice. Now all your needs have to be met by her.*" Meredith said with all the sadness of a death in the family.

"*I miss you. Don't you miss me? Have you stopped loving me already?*" I ask.

"*I miss your smile, your smell, sleeping next to you, watching movies with you, being silly with you, etc... You know I miss you. It's not my fault we are apart. Why do you want to know? Love didn't stop* what happened so what's love got to do with it now?" she remarks.

"*Just nice to hear it man. It doesn't make you feel good to know that I miss you?*" I ask.

"*To be honest, I don't know how it makes me feel. Or what it is supposed to mean.*" she retorts.

"*It means just what I say. I truly miss you; being around you, talking to you, all of it.*" I say.

"*I get that but you left me...are you supposed to miss me? It is kind of like you signed up for a life that would include missing me. I didn't choose it so I don't know where to put those feelings.*" she says.

"*You have left me before. It doesn't matter who left who. You can still miss that person. Especially when the people are as close as we were. I didn't lie to you, I love you. I think you feel the way you do because you believe I lied to you.*" I try to say convincingly.

"*Don't worry about whether or not I feel like you lied to me. It's my opinion that you lie to yourself wayyyyy more than you lie to me. Good night.*" she ends the call.

Well that went well, I think to myself sarcastically. I believe now is as good a time as any to get drunk. After getting off work, I head to the strip club. I go to the bar and order a Bud Lite with a Hennessy back. As I turn around a bump from someone makes the liquor careen off the side of the glass onto my light blue button down. I look up right into the chest of a big dude. I'm six feet, how tall is this dude? Better yet how wide is he? I can barely see around him. I look up to find the head of the eclipse only to be met with a mean mug.

"*What? Yeah I know you a cop but I bet you ain't so tough out of uniform.*" says the silverback, leaving me looking confused.

"*Look, I don't know you but I'm off duty tonight and I'm here to chill.*" I tell him.

"*You can chill, just go around me. You in MY way.*" he said in a daring manner as two other guys come to flank his left and his right.

As I shift my weight, I can see through the space between him and his buddy on his right side. My attention goes to the face of a familiar guy. Buddha was motioning for some the guys in his section to come my way. What a way to repay my generosity. These dudes work for him? If I make it out of this situation alive, Meredith's brother or not, he is going down.

It didn't take long for about 10 or 12 of Buddha's guys to make it to where we were standing by the bar. The crowd seems to part like the red sea as they move through. I turn my attention back to the big guy and just as I get ready to speak, I realize Buddha's crew gathers behind me.

"*Everything alright over here?*" one of the 12 asks, directing his question to me but sizing up the big guy.

Wait...I have back up! For the mood I was in, I could have easily just allowed this situation to blow up. Thank God I hadn't started drinking yet or I may have. Instead, I realize the immediate danger to the innocent bystanders and knew I had to get everything under control quickly.

"*I think if my new friend would move out of my path, we'd be finished here. What do you say new friend? Are we finished?*" I ask the big guy.

Amazing how the cat can get the tongue of even a guy this huge when the odds aren't in his favor. He says nothing but complies with my wishes and moves to the side pushing one of his partners out of the way to clear my path forward. After giving him a sideways smile, I begin to walk past him toward Buddha's table. Before I could get completely by him, he knocks my glass out my hand and tries to come back with a blow to my head with the back of his hand. Lucky dude is not fast, I duck out the way just in time as I contort my body to position myself behind him but facing his broad back. Before I knew it, in my next reaction I wrap my hand tighter around my beer bottle for a blow to the back of his head with my left hand giving the momentum for me to come around with a low blow to his right side with a closed fist from my right hand. As he stumbled, an all-out brawl ensues in front of me. Buddha's 12 guys engulf the big guy and his two sidekicks. People run from the bar stools as the scuffle twists like a tornado sending glasses and beer bottles alike hurling from the bar's surface. The crowd hurriedly scampers away from the circumference of the fight as it spirals out of control consuming everything in its path. The ball of destruction heads toward the front door as I follow half shocked and half on ready behind it. Joining my side as I go toward the door is Buddha. No words were exchanged, just our eyes making sure the fight didn't reach the exterior of the building without us close behind.

In the parking lot, Buddha gives the command for his guys to back away. As the ball turns into more of a donut with three battered and bruised heaps in the middle, I realize the totality of the situation. Hell are they even alive?

I motion for the head of security and request a call for an ambulance. As I turn back to the heap in the middle of the crowd, Buddha puts his hand on my shoulder.

"You have to trust me to take care of this because right now you can't be here." He said. Before I could turn away, he hands me an unopened Bud Lite and finished with, *"Aren't you forgetting something?"*

Well look how quickly backs are scratched and favors are repaid. I just smile and take the beer with a thankful nod. What a fucking day! Wheeeeeeeeew!

I open my eyes to see the sun streaming through the hole made by the lifted tape that used to affix my black curtains to the wall just beyond the window. I turn toward the clock on my cable box, it's 1pm. If I had to go to work after a night like last night, I definitely wouldn't make it. I get out of bed rubbing my head with one hand and adjusting my morning wood with the other. Even after the morning sprinkle to the toilet bowl, my member didn't seem to want to soften. Isn't this supposed to be the honeymoon period? Who gets engaged and doesn't get sex? That's my life. I wouldn't be Casey Canyon unless I was in some kind of bullshit.

Sam's excuse for not taking care of my sexual needs was that her trust issues wouldn't allow her to desire sex from me. If it's not one thing it's another with her. She has a host of demands of what she needs from me but she's not delivering shit for me right now. That motherfucker wouldn't get me a cup of juice if it was within her reach. Right when I am ready to give it all up for someone that runs an immaculate household and handles her business well, I remember I want her to stop finding fault with me and actually want to touch me too.

Clothes in baskets on the floor and dust on the ceiling fan but Meredith stayed with her body against mine, rubbing on me, making me feel like I was more than enough. She is a woman, so of course there is a complaint here and an emotional come apart there, nonetheless she saw me as imperfectly perfect for her. Sometimes she believed in me more than I believed in myself.

Carpe Diem, I think to myself as I send Meredith a text message, "Hey, I apologize if the conversation got too heavy yesterday. I just want our friendship back. Call me?" It didn't take long before she replied, "You changed your number so that I couldn't call you. You call me." She can't just give in without a smart remark. At least she gave in and that's all that counts.

"*Thanks for accepting my call. How are you?*" I start off.

"*Cut the pleasantries Casey. What's this about a friendship?*" she says sternly.

"*Okay, straight to the point, that works for me. Well I really want us to develop a friendship again. That's what made us strong and I believe that is what we need to rebuild.*" I declare.

"*Honestly Casey, I would love that. I don't just miss you, I miss us. However, I cannot be your friend if you are going to be with Sam. That is too much to ask of me given everything that has happened. You need to focus on the choice you made. You need to focus on Sam.*" she says in rebuttal.

"*All I've been doing is trying to focus on Sam. I really think I'm doing my part. Who knew one person* could be so insatiable? *She is never happy about anything unless she is putting on a front for other people. I think deep down she doesn't feel this will work either. She doesn't want me to touch her, let alone have sex. I think I'm ready to hang myself."* I say without realizing what I divulged.

"Don't hang yourself. I'll do it for you". After a short fit of laughter, she says *"But seriously, I'm not even angry with you anymore. I am just hurt, disappointed and frustrated. So I'm going to give you what I think is food for thought; you don't have to eat it. Think about why you are hanging on to considerations of marriage if it is clear it won't include the kind of friendship you think you need."*

"It may be hard to believe but I did come to a realization. I can live without Sam in my life. I cannot live without you Meredith." I confess.

After what seems like too long of a silence, I say hello to confirm she's still on the line.

"I'm here; it's just surprising that's all. So what made you come to that realization?" she asks, sounding as if she may even believe me.

"When I thought about you not being in my life and I thought about Sam not being in my life. To

be honest I would be sad not to have her in my life but I could live without her in it." I say emphatically.

"*Why can't you do without me in your life Casey?*" she asks through what I know are tears.

"*I guess because you are more than just a lover Meredith, more than just someone I could see myself being with for the rest of my life. You have become almost a part of me. The best way to describe it would be like living with only one arm or one leg. I don't feel whole without you in my life. When you said good bye yesterday like it was the end, like that was the final good bye, it made me think how I would feel if that happened? I've been thinking about it since the night at the karaoke bar but I really didn't realize what it meant to me until today. When I think about you I smile even after we argue. How can I have a person that makes me smile out of my life?*" I respond feeling drained but relieved at the same time.

"*If you look into my heart, what do you think you will see?*" she queries.

"*I think I will see me. Even through all the shit I put you through, I do believe that I'm still in your heart.*

Although I slept alone, I haven't slept that well in a while. What a difference a day makes. After another week, things weren't in line yet but I felt better than I had in at least a month. Meredith and I were back in regular communication. Sam and I were putting distance between each other. She had no idea I'd taken steps to get closer to Meredith but she did agree that her overall dissatisfaction with me did not make for an encouraging marriage.

I enjoy talking to Meredith during my shift like old times. We've pretty much communicated our way through the damage done at the karaoke bar. I haven't seen Buddha since the fight that night. But I never got the story of how he and Meredith became so close. After mentioning it, she explained she actually met him through a girl he dated at one time. He became her friend's boyfriend and he always treated them both well. After he and her friend broke up, she didn't see him anymore for years. One day he popped back up on the scene. Through conversation she learned he'd gone to prison for a bid on drugs and was back out on his feet again. Much like 2Pac, he went in slim and came out with a much bigger frame. He wasn't overly muscled but he clearly wasn't a small dude anymore. Becoming like family after many interactions, Buddha even financed Meredith during her tenure in school for her paralegal degree. I'm used to her creating family from strangers but their connection to one another was stronger than play cousins. They really act as blood siblings. Sacrificing and celebrating for and with each other as a barrier against a cruel world.

What I respect even more about Buddha from the background Meredith gave, is he didn't want her in his world. Aside from the occasional party, he discouraged and dare I say forbid her from interacting heavily in his circles. Everyone that knew Buddha also knew that she was his sister and everyone knew that meant she was off limits. With this astutely protective attitude, there's no wonder he knew who I was before I ever knew he existed. He took care of her like a brother should but if I were to be with her, he expected me to serve my position well.

They love each other and now thanks to me having proven myself, I am free to love her with his blessing. I look out for him within the guise of discretionary law enforcement powers. A fixed ticket here, a call to discourage detainment there but nothing too involved, until today.

External Affair

A little too flashy but I didn't have a reason to dislike him. - Casey

We are not the three amigos but Meredith, Buddha and I are definitely more associated. One of the few places Meredith is allowed to rub elbows in Buddha's world is at the Spot. Situated in a residential neighborhood, it looks like any house from the outside. On the inside the living room and dining room area are furnished as a small bar. Music plays as a card game goes on in the would-be living room, shit talking of a professional caliber goes on at the tables in the dining area while chicken and fish fries in the kitchen.

A detached garage in back of the house is reconstructed into a one bedroom efficiency apartment. Buddha sometimes spends the night there with the flavor of the month girl. That is until one flavor didn't know her month was up and tried to burn it down in a jealous rage. Now it just stands as a monument to Buddha's prowess and the occasional 'remember that crazy girl' joke.

On my first visit there, it didn't take long for me to realize the establishment was family run. One of Buddha's biological sisters, Callie, is the bartender. The prices are reasonable, she pours with a heavy hand and is deserving of every dollar smashed into her oversized brandy glass tip jar. In the kitchen is Momma. You can get a plate from her that is better than a meat and two from a restaurant for the price of a happy meal. Buddha's mother is beautiful. She clearly did not look old enough to have children in their 30s and older. Like her food, her service is excellent. Your presence in this little known location is validation enough for her to treat you like she's known you forever.

I didn't frequent the joint because the contact I get from being in there alone will have my continued employment denied if I'm ever administered a random drug test. I heard stories of when Meredith was in regular attendance a couple of years ago. They would all convoy down from the Spot to the club on amateur night, already buzzed and ready to party every week. At that time Meredith was sweet on a dude named T.J. Within Buddha's crew, he is a main supplier. He runs pills from California to Birmingham through some local chick there on the west coast. Not exactly ranked under Buddha, T.J. is a lateral which may explain why

Buddha did not interfere when a romantic thing brewed between he and Meredith. Even the fact that he dated her didn't bother me when I met him. She and I were off at the time they dated, I think I was into a stripper with the perfect combo of body and face. As a candidate for her, I didn't like T.J.'s chosen occupation but he seemed to shield her from the business end of it. Plus he is a pretty likable dude. I know him from coming in the club. He never gives me any trouble, just throws lots of cash at the stage and always pays a pretty high tab from buying drinks for himself and all those around him. A little too flashy but I don't have a reason to dislike him.

Back then I had no idea how this close degree of separation would impact me, would impact my job.

"*BRUH YOU HAVE TO COME DOWN THE STREET! THEY LEFT HIM IN THE ROOM AND BAILED!*" Buddha exclaims out of breath.

I answered my phone and didn't even have a chance to say hello before he began to speak. I'm not even sure I didn't miss some information because I don't know what the hell he is saying exactly.

"*Buddha where down the street are you?*" I ask.

"*T.J.! T.J.! COME ON MAN! SHIT CASEY, I THINK HE'S DEAD! HIS BRAINS ARE COMING OUT OF THE SIDE OF HIS HEAD!*" he responded.

I thought Buddha was still inside the club. It takes me a minute to make the connection that not only is he not in the club, but he'd left to meet T.J. somewhere close by. I get Buddha focused enough to tell me exactly which room he is in and at which hotel. Upon my arrival, at the Southern Comfort Motel just a few blocks away, a cluster fuck of bad news was waiting. Standing only a few feet from the closet, stood Buddha nervously smoking a cigarette. It was a cheap hotel and only used for meetings by the crew. By the looks of things, this meeting didn't go well.

"*What did you touch?*" I quickly ask Buddha. Assessing the situation, I realize there is a party going on next door and I don't know if any of the guests are potential witnesses. I've already taken too much discretion by coming down here and not calling the location in to dispatch.

As though he had to shake himself back into reality, Buddha answers, "*Nah, I didn't touch anything but the door. But I can't be here. I can't be a witness. I can't go to court.*"

"*I know but first I need you to tell me what happened.*

Buddha tells me the story. T.J. had arrived alone to the hotel in his own car. When he arrived on the hotel lot, he parked beside the car Buddha was in with two others in his crew. T.J. joins them sitting in the empty seat behind the driver's seat. This hotel is a small, crack head overrun spot. Each room had its own outside door that opened to the parking lot. A Tahoe drives up before T.J. could close the door to the car and a guy from the truck calls him over. T.J. gets out, closes the car door and motions for the guy to follow him into the room. Through the tinted windows of his car, Buddha could see that both of the guys from the truck were young, probably in their early 20s. However, since it was clear that T.J. knew the dudes, no one continued their attention beyond the hotel room door closing. It wasn't long before T.J. came back out to the car closing the door behind him this time. The guys got back in the truck and drove off the lot.

Before the blunt could complete a second rotation T.J. got a phone call and told everybody he'd be right back. As he shuffled like a penguin with his jeans waistband low on his hips toward the hotel room door, Buddha and the others continued the rotation. A few minutes later Buddha hears a gunshot from the room just before a vehicle burns rubber out the parking lot of the Express Oil next door. Buddha kicks in the hotel room door and finds T.J. propped up between the bed and the wall unit air conditioner where he apparently landed after his fall, with blood pouring from the side of his head. That is when he called me.

"Go ahead and go, I got this. I will call you later." I say, knowing damn well I didn't think I HAD anything. A minute after he drives off in the opposite direction of the club, I call the scene in to dispatch as I wipe Buddha's prints off the front door that was now wide open exposing the top half of T.J.'s lifeless body to passersby. I couldn't waste any more time, I'd have to think on my feet. The quicker detectives and a ground team got to work on this, the better the chance we could find out who did this.

After detectives claim the scene, they and more officers flood the outside of the hotel to gather evidence and ask questions. As if the half-witted explanation I gave as to how I came across the scene wasn't bad enough, word got around down at the club. Even after a crowd grows with party goers both from the hotel room next door to the scene and the club, no one would say much of anything to detectives. Everyone with anything to say came to me. As potential witness after hearsay provider filed in and out of my presence, it was noticeable to my brothers in blue that pieces to the puzzle they were trying to put together were being given to me and me alone.

"*Hey baby, I know it's late but what is Buddha's number to his private phone?*" I ask.

"*His private phone? What's going on?*" Meredith replies sleepily.

I let out a deep sigh before saying, "*I just need the number. I never programmed it.*"

"*Where is my brother Casey? Is he okay? What's going on?*"

I could never hide much from her, I think as I answer enough to get the information I need, "*Baby, I'm sorry to tell you this but T.J. is dead. Someone shot him. Buddha was here but I told him to leave and now I need to reach him.*"

She stammers through the digits of the number. I didn't have to see her face to know tears rolled down it. I ask her if she knew T.J.'s given name, it was amazing how many people knew him but couldn't give me his real name. After writing down Thomas Johnson then assuring her I would call her back when things calmed down, we hung up. Buddha didn't answer the line but we wouldn't have been able to talk anyway. As I pull my cell from my face, an older woman supported by two younger men on either side of her approach me.

"*Are you Officer Canyon?*" she asks.

I confirmed and she introduced herself as Mrs. Mary Davis, T.J.'s mother. After speaking with the family and only divulging some basic facts, I look up in time to see an Internal Affairs officer standing with the homicide detectives and all looking over at me. The I.A. officer may have missed the circus of everyone coming to me to give what they felt was case solving information but this display with the family didn't give me angel wings. As I excuse myself from the family, I remind myself that I cannot control who people feel comfortable giving information to and walk over to the detectives.

"*This is all the information I was given tonight along with the contact information of the people willing to give it to me. I apologize for the circumstances, I've worked the Palace as an extra job so long, I guess the patrons just feel more comfortable coming to me.*" I explain as I hand them all my notes that do not include mention of Buddha.

"And what is your full name and employer number Officer Canyon?" the I.A. requested with a look of discontentment on his face.

Despite the homicide detectives' feelings of disrespect toward the way they were ignored and personal discomfort in my being given the information they pursued, there wasn't anything I.A. could make a case out of against me. But now I was on their radar and anything with my name on it that came across their desk from here out would not manifest support on their part.

By the time I arrive at Meredith's place, her eyes are bloodshot and the usually light skin on her face is rose colored under her poodle curly hair.

"I'm sorry this happened to your friend baby. He was an alright guy." I say as I embrace her in a comforting hug. *"Have you heard from Buddha?"*

"Yes, I talked to him. He's laying low at Hitch's house. Not many people know they are friends so no one will figure he is there. " she says.

Meredith lay on my chest and cries until the sun came up. Eventually she falls asleep but I'm still up. I'm wide awake, going over my cover story in my head. My eyes are wide open as I replay the early morning events in my head like a movie, a movie I wish I wasn't a character in at all.

It only took a few days for me to be questioned on my official report of my involvement in the investigation with T.J.'s death. By now, I could confidently recant a believable story. After a little investigation of my own, I found out the other hotel room beside the scene was vacant and none of the guests from the side the party was on had seen anything before police cars showed up to the scene. No one could refute my account of what happened before I called the location in to dispatch. Even if I was given sideways glances by some of those in the department, I was definitely free from any misconduct charges.

I stay my distance but check on Buddha through Meredith for a while, just in case. Luckily the phone he called me from that night was a burner and therefore could not be linked to him. He had since gotten rid of the phone and was laying low on coming in the club too. Just like the saying the show must go on, so must business. With Hitch as the new point man on supplies, it didn't take long for T.J.'s absence to be filled. It is personal to mourn a death but it is business to replace a missing link in the flow of money. Although the stripper proclaiming to be his last girlfriend got T.J.'s name tattooed on her, not even her allegiance will be forever. Even she will go on with life without him.

"*I thought you said you were coming over?*" I hear in my phone immediately after saying hello.

"*It'll be late, I have a few things to take care of first. I told you I'm still dealing with loose ends from this case and yes Meredith, but I'll be there.*" I say, hoping to prevent hearing a rant.

"*You know what, I have replayed this thing over and over in my head and I just don't get it. You knew from the beginning you were not going to work on what I need from you. Why did you bring me back into this if you knew that you were not going to let it be just us? Why are you still trying to be around with her? I know why you won't close that door. You don't have to tell me, you show it. I have talked to you as much as I can and told you how I feel about this but that doesn't matter. When you love someone, no one can come between that…. you love her and I can't come between that! There is nothing else for me to do Casey. Like I told you yesterday, this is not the first time you put her before me. Now I see why she hangs around, she knows you aren't going anywhere. You telling me the truth about still being friends with her was not because you didn't want to keep lying to me, it was because you knew it all was going to come out sooner or later. I don't know why I kept ignoring the fact that you will always be the way you are when it comes to her! I really thought you wanted this with me. If this was what you wanted, you would have let her go and we wouldn't be going through this bullshit. You didn't and you will not let her go!"* Sam rants anyway before hanging up in my face.

Hitch-hiker

"It is a twist on the old saying big fish in a little pond." - Hitch

I walked into the apartment and the first thing I see is a huge fish tank set into the wall. Who does this dude think he is? I half expect to see a neon "The World Is Mine" sign lit up somewhere. I laugh to myself right before being greeted by Buddha and Hitch.

"*Nice crib dude, it's very you.*" I say to Hitch.

I've only seen Hitch a hand full of times. Besides being Buddha's new supplier, I don't have a kinship with the dude. He's cool enough because he seems to fulfill his obligations to Buddha on the up and up. Something is a little off about him; call it my spidey senses tingling.

The guy that opened the door for me was Marcus, one of Buddha's closest lieutenants. He was now returning to his seat at the table with Buddha, Hitch and another guy I didn't know. I guess I interrupted the card game and the shit talking.

Buddha laughs before saying, "*Casey knows how it is. He is an expert on such matters.*"

"*Man what you talking about bruh?*" I ask for clarification.

"*We talking about love triangles. It seems Hitch here got caught slipping with his account logged in and his main thang went through his Facebook messages. Now she is 38 hot because Hitch been sweet talking one of his ex-classmates and even told this woman he loves her. Sound familiar?*" Buddha laughed loudly.

"*Yeah but I am not announcing any marriages though homie.*" Hitch said looking at me.

"*Oh you familiar with grown man happenings? I thought you'd be busy trying to baggie up some aspirins.*" I say as a response to the snide remark.

"*Fellas, Fellas.*" Buddha says laughingly.

"*I didn't mean no disrespect man. I know you got all your business straight now. If I had a Meredith, I'd get my shit together too.*" Hitch interrupts.

"*No harm, no foul...if I can get one of those cold Bud Lites*" I say as I take a seat on the couch.

His words echoed in my head, "get my shit together". I wish I had my shit together. It's only a matter of time before this thing with Meredith and Sam comes to a head again. Right as Buddha sat beside me on the couch and hands me a cold one, my phone rings. We both looked at the screen in time to see Sam's picture popsnight up.

"*HA! The plot thickens.*" Buddha says as he looks at me amused. "*Hitch deal me in, my man might need to get his thoughts together.*"

I don't even address Buddha's acknowledgement of having recognized the caller, I just step out on the balcony to answer the call.

"*Hey baby, I might be a little longer than I thought. Do you need me to bring you anything?*" I say as sweetly as possible, hoping for a quick call.

"*What would I need that late? Hell I will be sleep. You may as well not come.*" Sam says just before I hear the beep of our disconnected call.

Well I said I wanted it quick, I thought as I shook my head. After a deep sigh I come back inside, sliding the balcony door behind me. As I pick my beer bottle up off the coffee table, I look once again at the fish tank. It is well lit and its glow fills the living room. These must be exotic fish because I haven't seen anything like most of them. I turn my attention toward the card game. I always get a small sense of déjà vu when I look at Hitch. I don't know where I could know him from but there is a tone of familiarity about him.

"*Where you get these fish from dude? A few of them even look like mini sharks.*" I say to draw Hitch into conversation.

"*Yeah those are Bamboo Sharks. They are small sharks; the adults don't get any longer than 48 inches. It is a twist on the old saying big fish in a little pond.*" Hitch responds looking me straight in my eyes.

"*If I didn't know any better, I'd think that was a personal insult directed at me. But why would that be? I don't have anything you want......or do I?*" I respond thinking back to his comment about Meredith.

"*Y'all killing my vibe. Let's take a walk baby boy.*" Buddha interrupts and points me toward the door before things can get too heated.

I squint my eyes at Hitch, studying his movements as he breaks eye contact with me to check out his hand for the next round of cards. To be continued I think to myself as Buddha guides me out the door.

"*Don't pay H no mind Casey. He got a few more dollars in his pockets these days and he's feeling himself.*" Buddha says in response to the tension.

"*Actually in addition to them dollars in his pockets, it seems he wants Meredith in his bed. I knew something was off about him but I didn't take him as the hater type.*" I speculate as I duck down into my car.

"*All I know is he good at what I need him to be good at and that's bring that product in on the regular without missing a beat.*" Buddha says.

"*I get ya' bruh, but a man that shows he wants what someone else has doesn't stop at one somebody, it's just one facet of his general motivation. Watch your back.*" I warn before driving off.

I don't know if the seed I planted in Buddha's head was a fair warning for him or just a backbiting response from me. Either way, I will be watching this Hitch dude more closely. Instead of dealing with another smart ass and going to Sam's place, I detour to Meredith's.

Using my key to come through the door, I hear Meredith on the phone. "*Oh that's kind of you but I'm sure Casey will take care of it when he gets around to it. Ah... speak of the devil, here he is now. Thanks again for that, good-bye.*"

"*Who was that?*" I ask.

"*Oh that was H, he heard me say something to Callie about her new barstools when I was at the Spot last time. He happened to see some for sell somewhere and asked if I wanted him to get them for me. I know it has been a minute since I mentioned them to you but I am sure you will get them as you promised. Maybe you can ask him where he saw them? I thought you said you'd be with them tonight? Hitch said you just left.*"

Oh this dude going in for the kill. I see shit is about to get real between he and I. Not only is he trying to wiggle in with Meredith by offering her attention and gifts, this bastard tried to hang me out to dry. If I would have gone to Sam's like originally planned, then thanks to his little information

Meredith would have known I left his house early. As soon as I'd have said I was with the fellas all night, she would have known I was lying. Touché motherfucker but this is a game you cannot win.

I come out of my thoughts to answer, "*Hey to you too baby. I thought I'd have better company here with you so I left. Don't worry about your barstools, you know I have to keep my favorite person happy. So how often does Hitch call you anyway?*"

"*Not often, I mean we talk but not like every day. He's an alright guy. You hungry?*" she responds.

"*I guess I didn't know y'all talked at all on the phone. I'm just surprised that's all. I haven't figured this guy out yet. Do me a favor and keep your distance until I do. Okay?*"

"*Ooooooookay, is there something wrong?*"

"*Like I said, I haven't figured it out yet. Go ahead and warm me up something, I'm going to jump in the shower.*" I say to drive my point home as softly as possible as not to raise anymore suspicions but I can tell Meredith wasn't really buying it.

In the shower the water was hot and the steam was thick. All I could think of was the nerve of this dude. He's just a supplier, Buddha can find another supplier. This dude has got to go and I'm going to find a way to help him along. I step out the bathroom in a stride that if it were just a bit slower, the plate of food would have hit my head instead of the wall behind me.

"*What the fuck?!*" I look toward Meredith and she has my phone in her hand. I instantly realize that with the distraction of this Hitch nonsense, I'd left my phone on the bed when I undressed to get in the shower.

"*As if "The Lady In My Life" ringtone wasn't a big enough clue, Sam's picture and name popped up as the caller. But I'm so stupid, I really just want to believe you didn't change all that shit after we got back together. But THIS: 'If I was not distracted by Meredith maybe I could have worked harder at our relationship. It was never my intention to hurt you and yes I did love you Sam. I still do.' Well let me stop distracting your love for Sam. GET THE FUCK OUT CASEY!!!*" Meredith screams.

I stood in disbelief only a second before my phone came hurling through the air but this time it hits its target, center mass in my chest. I immediately thought about a saying I'd heard all my life, when you dig a hole for someone else, you're actually digging one for yourself. No amount of reversal about why was she even in my phone would work to turn this in my favor. I was dead wrong and there was too much evidence to that fact. All I could do was get dressed as quickly as I could while avoiding looking at her as she cried and yelled. All I could do now was leave.

****

"*Well is she alright? She won't answer any of my calls and I don't want to just pop up over her house but I am starting to feel like I may need to do just that.*" I say.

"*She's alright bruh. She just doesn't want to talk to you man. She doesn't want to see you. The mere mention of your name sends her into a rage or tears, you just never know which one these days. I know you love my sister, but just leave her alone man. It's for the best right now.*" Buddha responded as he ended the call, giving me no chance at a rebuttal.

I wish things were that simple but they never are in reality. I grabbed my keys, got in the car and headed to Meredith's apartment. When I pulled up a lump formed in my throat as I see Hitch's Lexus parked in a space just yards from the concrete steps that lead up to the breezeway. As I walk up the steeper steps leading to her apartment door on the second floor, I am hoping my key still works after a month of her not speaking to me. I quietly insert the key then twist the knob and push at the same time opening the door with great force.

"*Where is he?!*" I yell through the apartment having not even spotted Meredith yet. I go toward the bedroom scared and ready at the same time for what I might see, but nothing. There is no one here I realize as I come out of the bathroom. On my way back through to the living room, I see the new barstools and then the front door I left flung wide open. I close the door and sit on the couch. What the hell am I going to do? There may not be any coming back from this. I might actually have to let go this time. I decide to just leave. Walking down the steps to my car, I look right into Meredith's face with a look of disbelief on it as she stands in the parking lot. I quicken my steps but she immediately gets back into her car to drive off. As I reach the curb, she has already backed out and is headed out of the apartment complex. I cannot tell if there is someone in the car with her or not although I strain to see. My first instinct is to follow her but I have done enough. I would never be able to explain to Buddha that something happened to her after I decided to chase her through the streets of Birmingham.

At work I am a zombie from lack of sleep. By now Meredith has changed her phone number. I don't dare ask Buddha for the new number, he has made it clear that he is not getting into the middle of her and me. I torture myself by riding by her apartment sometimes just to see what I can see, which most of the time is nothing. Every once in a while I will send her an email. 'I know that you are not going to respond to my emails and that's ok but I will continue to email you about things I think you would want to know about. If you would like me to stop just let me know and I will.' After weeks of no response, I finally get one:

Casey,

I'm gone.

~Meredith

What the hell does that mean? I call Buddha but he doesn't answer. Who else can I call? In that moment I realize I hadn't taken the time to get to know Meredith's friends, I just spoke and moved on. I didn't know any of her family well outside of Buddha. Before I realized it, my fingers were dialing the number.

"*Hello.*" the male voice greets.

"*Where is Meredith?*" I ask.

As he pulls his face away from the phone, I hear Hitch tell her that this call was for her.

"*Hello.*" she says.

"*Meredith? Where are you? What do you mean you're gone?*"

"*I am gone Casey. That is all you need to know. I didn't have to tell you anything. We are not even friends anymore. I don't owe you anything. Good-bye.*"

Hitch gets back on the phone, "*Hey man, I'm just being a friend trying to make sure she is alright. I don't mean to...*"

Remembering that is how she and I started off, I interrupt him, "*Friend huh? Just remember this: you can't take T.J.'s place in everything. Even he was just a distraction at best and never competition for me with Meredith.*"

The line went dead.

Downs & Ups

"You just can't be beating on everybody, man...You used to know stuff like that." - Big Rome

I finally stopped emailing Meredith, it was clear she was not going to respond. Even Hitch has changed his number. Buddha, true to his words, is still staying out of it. All he will tell me is that she is fine. I have not seen Hitch around so all I can think is that where ever she is, he is too. I have lost that battle. The best way to get over a woman is to get under another one or four. With the new crop of strippers imported into the club, I wasn't short on options. Thanks to video vixens and World Star Hip Hop breakout stars, most of the new strippers fit the same mold: thick in the hips, small in the waist and nothing over a mouth full in the chest. Everybody was a Jhonni Blaze replica. Every Jhonni Blaze replica could get this dick. Life was but a big party.

My monthly numbers on tickets and arrests went up on the job. I no longer show leniency in dealing with perpetrators, if you break the law you get a ticket or go to jail. Life is not being fair to me, why should I help others get over? My Internal Affairs Department complaints went up too. I seem to always be called in for this complaint or that complaint but I'm just doing my job. Of course criminals do not like it when the police do their job.

At the club, it didn't pay to give me any trouble. If I tell a dude not to sit on the stage or touch a stripper, then he needs to comply immediately or he is thrown out of the club with great force. Tonight would be no different. I don't know what this particular dude had on his mind, but I am not going to ask him again to get his beer bottle off the edge of the stage. As soon as I saw him replace the bottle on the edge of the stage with a 'fuck the police' comment added for good measure when he thought I didn't hear, I just went off. I drag the dude by his coat toward the door. When he starts to resist, I pull out my nightstick and beat him until he stops. I pull him the rest of the way out of the club and dump him to the ground of the parking lot.

"*Fuck this shit man! It ain't take all that! Wait until I...*" the dude says before I interrupted him with a kick to the stomach.

"*Oh y'all think you can just come in the club and do whatever you want, huh? It's fuck the police, huh? Well who getting fucked now?*" I exclaim as I continue to kick him wherever my boot lands.

Big Rome pulls me off him and says, "*Come on man. He's out the club now, just let him go.*"

Some guys come over and help the dude up off the ground and into a car nearby. After they drive off, I look at Big Rome who is looking back at me with a concerned expression. I drop the scowl on my face as the crowd dissipates.

"*What man?*" I ask him.

"*You just can't be beating on everybody, man. That was Councilman Berry's son. That lil dude don't mean no harm. He just likes to flex because of who his daddy is to this city. You used to know stuff like that.*" Rome says as he walks off shaking his head.

This is bullshit. Rome may have to deal with that kind of thing being head of security, but I am the police. You do not disrespect the police. That goes against the grand order of things. Even little punks need to be taught that, especially when your daddy didn't teach you. It was a short night after that. The crowd at the club died down and those left didn't so much as throw trash on the floor. No problems, just like I like it.

It took less than a week for this Councilman Berry's son shit to blow up in my face. My Internal Affairs interview was a mere formality; they had already decided there would be a determination hearing. Charges of conduct unbecoming of an officer, failure to arrest, excessive force and others are looming over my head. I know fellow police officers that continued to beat perpetrators while they were unconscious and another that beat the shit out of perpetrators while in handcuffs, there is no way they were going to give me more days off without pay than they gave to them. Working at the club every Friday, Saturday and Sunday, I have a good cushion saved up. Give me a month off, I'll go chill in Miami. I haven't been to the King of Diamonds since that year Meredith and I were in Miami for the Pro Bowl.

Meredith….there is a name I have managed to keep out of my head for a little while. Meredith…. she would be pissed if she were here. I am not even sure if she would recognize who I am now. I'm not too sure that I recognize who I am now.

After getting my ass chewed at the determination hearing, it was obvious I was not going to get out of this situation unscaved. They seem to be out for blood. I picked the wrong time to commit such an offense. After the department has had to deal with an officer charged with rape, three officers up on arson charges and one in a very public domestic violence case; their public reputation is under a lot of scrutiny. Up to three days is given after a determination hearing to be informed of what your punishment will be but I just received notice that they are taking an extension that gives them up to ten more days. Anybody that has been informed of an extension in the past NEVER got good news at the end of the ten days. On top of that, word around the department is that my neck is in the guillotine because Councilman Berry is slated to be the next Mayor and therefore the Chief's next boss. I will be made an example of for my offenses for sure.

As a precaution, I stop working at the club but I did not stop going to the club. If I ever needed strippers and booze, it was now. I see Buddha every now and then. He will buy me a drink or two and send over a private dance from a fine stripper but we don't really talk. Tonight is the first time we actually had a conversation.

"Bruh, I hear things are getting tough." Buddha says as he sits beside me.

"*Yeah, I hear the same.*" I say with a short laugh but without taking my eyes off the stripper slowly hypnotizing me with her full hips.

"*Look, I never doubted that you love my sister. It is not my business but it seems to be tearing you up bruh. If you do not get it together, you could lose a lot before it all blows over.*" he says.

I look to the ground and I finally summon the words to say, "*I did not mean to hurt her again, I hope you know that Buddha.*"

"*It is what it is man but now you got problems, bigger problems than her. I can help but I need you to lay low. Do your shift without any ordeals and stay out of this club. Night life is not for you right now. If you do that, you will see better days sooner than you think.*" he says as he gets up to leave.

I do just as Buddha told me. I work my shift. I patrol my beat and do my job. My nights are now mostly filled with Call of Duty and God of War. I have even started back running. I had forgotten how much running was therapeutic to me. I was a self-proclaimed track star in high school with Olympic hopes halted by an injury. That time was one of the highlights of my life. Oh how the mighty falls.

I now spend a lot more time around my family. I need that father figure in my uncle right now. His law enforcement experience is probably the reason I decided to get into law enforcement in the first place. I respect this man more than most men. When our conversation turns to integrity and the importance of doing the right thing, I feel like I have let him down. He stresses that when you do the right thing, you are more at peace because you lack the stress that comes with the other foot dropping when you do the wrong thing. I know it is my decisions that have gotten me into this mess on my job and in my personal life.

I still see Sam from time to time but as usual every time introduces new arguments, even after I stopped going through strippers by the dozens. Her high strung personality never brings the peace of mind I crave. Right now, I need as much peace as I can get. I guess it is just the quiet before the storm. It is almost time for judgment day.

I am nervous of course. I stand as the doors to where the hearing was being held are opened. The young man that walked out looked familiar. He smiled directly at me as he passed. At the behest of the guy holding the door open, I enter the room. I take a seat up front. I'm trying to look at the panel in front of me to determine my fate by the looks on their faces. One of the duty chiefs begins to talk. "*In light of the statement of one Erik Parsons, a witness of the events of the night in question and friend to Gavin Berry, the alleged victim, Officer Casey Canyon has been cleared of all charges except failure to arrest. We shouldn't have to remind you that once you engage a perpetrator and use force, they must be taken into custody.*"

Oh my God, did he just say what I thought he said? My celebratory thoughts were so loud, I almost missed hearing the three day suspension handed down to me by the panel. Hell I will take it. That is definitely a walk in the park compared to what I was up against. As soon as I get to my car, I call Buddha.

"*Bruh, where did you find this Erik kid? I can't believe what just happened!*"

"*Everything turned out to your satisfaction I suppose?*" Buddha laughs.

"*I can do those three days with my eyes closed, satisfaction isn't the word! So who was the kid?*"

"*A while back you helped out a kid that was driving his brother's car with drugs in it. It happens that kid is friends with Gavin Berry and was there that night you beat the shit out of him. He felt he owed you."*

"Wait, what? Mannnn I remember that kid now. How did you even know about him?"

"I didn't but Meredith did."

"Meredith?"

"Yeah Meredith. I don't want to be in the middle of whatever you call this thing you guys have but I knew she would never forgive me if you were in this kind of trouble and I didn't tell her. She came up with finding the boy."

"I want to talk to her, can you arrange that?"

"You know how she is but I will try. Hey look bruh, I have to go but I will get up with you later. Congratulations."

Even from wherever she is, this woman is still having a positive impact on my life. I cannot expect her to be all forgiving even if she cared enough to still have a hand in protecting me. I'm still thinking about her and the fantasy that would be me and Meredith together as I run the hills up and down through my apartment complex the next day. I do not have much time before I have to be at roll call for another shift. Despite all I have gone through, I love my job. I guess recent events show I need to act like I would like to keep it.

Fresh off roll call and in my squad car, I get a call from Buddha.

"*Hey Bruh, what are you doing this weekend?*"

"*I don't have anything on the calendar. What's up?*"

"*How about a little time away? Since you don't have anything to do this weekend, I got a little road trip for you. You'll be back in time to clock-in after the weekend.*"

"*Sounds like just what the doctor ordered. Where to?*"

"*Just a little sun, beach and honeys in bikinis. I'll swing the itinerary by later.*"

"*Cool, thanks bruh.*"

I don't know how he knew but I needed this down in my soul. By the description he gave I thought my destination would be Miami but I guess that does not fit with the plan of me staying out of trouble or strip clubs. I have never been to nor heard of Sandestin, Florida. But is there a bad part of Florida off of water? A lot of things drift through my head as I take the drive down to Florida but mostly I take in the sights. Funny how the air and even the sky seems to change as you get closer to the ocean, just the drive dissolves layers of every day stress. The accommodations aren't beachfront but the bright yellow condos weren't too shabby.

After check-in, I go up to the condo and put my bags just inside the door then turn to give myself a self-guided tour of the grounds. The condos are right on Baytown Wharf. The wharf is where everyone seemed to gather. Along with the booths manned by salesman with tempting offers if you just sit through an hour presentation for a timeshare, there are plenty of restaurants and shopping spots. I see an old favorite and walk right toward Fat Tuesdays. A frozen alcoholic treat would be a great kick off to this little vacation. I wonder in and out of shops with odd gifts, personalized gifts, toys and more. I quickly realize this would be a great spot for a couple to relax. That thought takes a little of the fun out of my tour so I decide to go back to the condo. I bet once the sun sets, the nightlife in this place will be a little more to my liking.

As I approach my condo door, I hear jazz pouring from under the door. Did I leave a radio on? As I push the door open, I am almost bowled over at the sight. Standing there in a red sundress and a tan that would make a Greek god jealous was Meredith. I always did love red against her skin. I always did love her.

Sandestiny

"I deserve a lot of things but I'm not sure I deserved this." - Casey

I didn't know whether to kiss her, pull her toward the bedroom or what, so I just stand there and take in the scenery. The room opens up onto a balcony. On the balcony it appeared food and wine glasses awaits a lucky couple. Was I included in this couple? My eyes go back up to Meredith.

"I've seen you speechless like when I found out you were still with Sam but I don't think I have ever seen you speechless in a good way. I take it the accommodations are to your liking sir?" she says.

"I, I, I...." I stutter when she begins to speak again.

"I guess you would like to know what is going on? I think that is a fair question. What is going on Mr. Canyon, is that we have a lot to talk about and I figured we could do that better without distractions...oh there goes that word again" she says

with a roll of her eyes. "*I feel it will be more productive away from home.*"

"*I have to admit that I am thrown off guard. I did not know you would be here. I am confused. Do you forgive me? Is this OUR room?*"

"*I have to admit that I want to forgive you but this is not our room, this is your room.*"

"*I understand. I am all for talking.*"

"*Good we will start with dinner.*" she says as her arms invite me to the balcony like a game show girl invites you to peruse the prizes.

I notice my luggage has been neatly tucked into the closet. I also couldn't help but to see Meredith used the kitchen to whip up whatever we are about to eat. As I approach the table I see and smell some sort of smothered chicken dish. She was always good at finding recipes that sounded weird but tasted good. I pull out her chair for her to have a seat and she did. I sit across from her and as I grab my silverware, she says grace.

"*Lord thank you for the food before us, the hands that prepared it and the mouths that will eat it. Please bless Casey and me with civil conversation and open hearts. Amen.*"

I take a deep breath as I think amen. I stare at the plate before me then I am urged to begin eating by the movements of Meredith beginning her meal.

"We started as friends. We were friends an entire year before we started dating. That is how we got to know each other so well. We were honest and we told each other everything. With all that has happened, I don't think we ever really rebuilt that friendship after the fight between Sam and I. We are no longer friends and we don't act like friends. I have come to the realization that no matter how much of a selfish bastard you are, I love you. I don't love anyone the way that I love you. But we have to be friends first. Our friendship is what connected us with a special bond. We have to find it again."

"I can agree with that. It is what we were supposed to be doing when we got back together" I say with my head low from the weight of having let her down so much.

"I never saw it as a competition of who is better, she or I. She's smart, I'm smart...hell we may have even been friends in a past life. You claim you value peace of mind but you have always complained that you two argue all the time even before I came back into the picture. Obviously we both have positive things in our favor or you wouldn't want to

be with both of us. I am about to do the hardest thing I've ever done and ask you, what does she have that I don't? How can I be enough for you?"

A little startled by the question, I realize I cannot give her the answer she is looking for without hurting her. What Sam has despite her crazy ways, Meredith cannot reproduce. Just as Sam could not be like Meredith even if she wanted to, no matter how hard she tried.

"I don't want you to be Sam. I want you to be you. It is my fault really, I have this image of a perfect woman and I have to live like I know that image is not reality. It's just hard to let go of and that makes it hard for me."

"There is so much of myself I do not give to you because I don't feel you giving me all of you. How do you know whether or not I could complete more of your needs if you do not ever work to earn it from me? You cannot expect me to give you my best while you are dividing your best between two people."

"You say you want to be friends and as friends we were honest with each other right? Well, let's talk as friends and be honest. It was never my intention to hurt either of you but I was comfortable with you AND Sam. It made a total life for me, having you

both. I can tell you right now that I want to be with just you and mean it. But truth be told, I have meant it every time I have said it to you. The problem is I do not know if I can get Sam completely out of my system. I know now it all boils down to the kind of person I want to be; who I am when I am with you. I can be myself. But that does not stop me from wanting her. No one understands me like you do. But that does not stop me from messing it up. I am not saying it is fair, I am saying it is where I am right now. I may not always be like this, but it is who I am now. I'll have to teach myself how to be the kind of man that you have always told me I can be. I wish I had as much faith in me as you do."

"So in this DMX let a dog roam and that dog will come back home philosophy, what am I supposed to be doing exactly?"

"I can't answer that for you Meredith. I cannot expect you to wait while I get my shit together. I know it is too much to ask but I have my plate filled with the things I need to do. I cannot tell you what you should do."

With tears in her eyes, she says "Well isn't that just great. I've had enough for one night."

I stand as she stands but I don't stop her from leaving. As I sit back down I see she didn't eat a lot from her plate just as I had not done so from mine. But I welcome the breeze that touches my face and arms as I watch the moon reflect off the pool outside of the balcony. As my stomach lets out a growl, I turn my attention back to the chicken. After completing my meal, I bring everything inside. I clean the kitchen to the sound of ESPN in the background. When I arrived I'd thought I would spend the evening on the wharf. Now, I will let the loop of sports information replay on ESPN every 20 minutes watch me sleep.

The sun filling the room, I open my eyes to a better view of the gardenlike pool area just outside the balcony from my window. I sit up straight to have my wonderment interrupted by dishes clanging in the next room. I walk into the kitchen to find Meredith pulling croissants out of the oven.

"Good morning. I didn't expect to find you here."

"I did not arrange for you to come here to leave it like we did last night. I figure we will try again today. But after we eat and we have a little fun."

After breakfast we catch a ride from the shuttle to rent bikes. We ride the bikes around the resort past the golf course and bungalow housing then along the main street before stopping at a spot with benches on our journey back. As we sit and just take in the sights, I enclose her hand in mine and to my surprise she doesn't take it away. We sit in silence until she suggests we complete the trip to take the bikes back. After taking the shuttle to return to the wharf, we go to The Village Door for lunch and then to a few of the shops before going back to the condo. I made a mental note of her like of the Barefoot Princess and CoCo & Company stores. Before she leaves, this time with a smile instead of tears, she tells me to be ready at 7pm for a dinner cruise.

I figured on the cruise we would begin talking about our present situation again but what happened I did not expect. Meredith, in my arms as we overlook the bay while the SunQuest docked after dinner, tells me that she'd slept with Hitch to hurt me. I don't move a muscle. My first instinct is to push her over the edge but how can I after all I have done. I will have to take this in stride but got damn if I don't hate that guy enough as it is, now this. I remain silent.

The picture she and I had taken before boarding the Sunquest was now ready for purchase. She looked beautiful and I looked happy but now all I saw was her fucking Hitch. I was still quiet on the way to the condo. We walk hand and hand from the dock and as my thoughts drifted to him penetrating her, my grip got a little stronger. I was crushing her hand before I realized it.

"Ouch, that hurts Casey." she says.

"I didn't mean to hurt you Meredith but did you have to do that? Did you have to fuck him? I mean I didn't think that you didn't fuck him but for you to confirm it is just..."

"I didn't have to but after what you did, I wanted to. He isn't even my type but I wanted you to hurt like you hurt me. I debated on even ever telling you. I know you must have imagined that he and I were together all this time but actually after he dropped me off at the airport, I never saw him again. He calls but I hardly ever talk to him. He thinks it is because of you that I don't want to be with him anymore but the truth is, it was because of you that I ever was with him. I did not want to admit to him that I used him. I did not want to admit it to you either."

"I deserve a lot of things but I'm not sure I deserved this."

"I know it was not the answer to the problem but you pushed me too far. You put me through the same shit just one time too many. So I wanted to hurt you back. The messed up part about it is, after I did it I realized how hurt you would be and I didn't even want you to know. In fact, I prayed you wouldn't find out."

"Well I know now."

"Yes you do. Since we are working on the friendship, I did not want it to seem like you were the only one that did something wrong. I did too. I just want to try and start from here. I can't do it by myself."

"I guess like you said, we start with the friendship. We start from here." I say as I drop her hand.

Those were the last words spoken until we got to the condo. Once inside, I turn to lock the door. As I turn back, Meredith is standing right in front of me.

"I'm sorry baby." she says as she kisses me.

My head isn't caught up to what is happening yet but my lips know what to do. They miss her and it is not the only part of my body that becomes conscious of her nearness, my member gets hard as a rock. I am not sure if it is okay to touch her until with her eyes still closed, her lips still embraced in our kiss, she drops the sundress from her shoulders. She has done enough; I will take it from here.

A great night and a great beginning to this friendship thing is all I can think when I awake with her laying on my chest. I cannot help but think this is how it is supposed to be; exactly how I am supposed to wake up and start my days. Pulling away from Sam for good will be harder than a crack head trying to quit in one day but I will have to do it if this is what I want.

Meredith filled in the gaps for me over breakfast. She has been living with family members in Jersey since she left. She just needed time to think but will be moving back to Birmingham soon. She promises we will keep in touch. She also promises that as long as I did my part to rebuild the friendship then she will do her part too. I cannot ask for more than that. I have to hit the road in order to make it back in time for work but I close my eyes as if to capture a picture of her lightly freckled face,

Caucasian nose, light brown eyes and near mocha skin before driving away.

The drive back seemed all too fast as I left my Meredith behind by more and more miles. Life will be better though and I look forward to it. As promised, Meredith and I talk a lot while she is still in Jersey. I will not say that I am officer of the year but I am doing my part on the job and I have even gotten involved with the Fraternal Order of Police Association. My uncle gave me encouragement after telling me how proud he is of my turn around.

"I'm giving you til tomorrow to do what you have to do to be with ME. If you can't..... then I'll know I was right and you love her not me! Me having to say anything about this is already showing me most of what I already know. You should want to make this work if you wanted it and remove anything that is coming between us if I am what you want. I just want you to prove me wrong for the first time."

Just like the others, this text message from Sam will also go unanswered. So far so good, life with Meredith is too good to mess it up for a final time. She will be on her way back from Jersey soon. We both feel our friendship is back intact. I feel it is time for the next step and I want her to move in with me.

I see a missed call from Buddha but I will call him back after my shift. I think taking him out for a drink or two would be appropriate. After all, I don't think I would be this happy without him having my back.

My shift was fairly easy, a few tickets and a watchful eye on a warehouse that had been broken into not long ago. With my mind in the right place these days, I even applied for a transfer to a detective position. After my interview I got good vibes. Unlike the last time there was buzz about me around the department, this time it was all good. I hear I am a shoe in to the Major Fraud unit. It will not mean more money except for overtime opportunities, but it will mean better work hours. Working office hours is better for a man trying to get back with his lady and build a life.

I don't know this number calling me and I don't usually answer numbers I do not know, but today is a good day.

"*Hello is this Casey?*" the voice asks.

"*Yeah, who is this?*" I answer.

"*Buddha needs you to come to the Spot like now man. Something's happened and he's been shot.*

He won't let nobody take him to the hospital man, and it looks bad. He's bleeding everywhere."

The Bad & The Ugly

"After Meredith left he was on some crazy shit." - Marcus

I ran every red light and cut off every car in my way. I almost had no less than three accidents before I made it to Buddha. He was lying across the couch with his mother holding a towel to his torso. I couldn't tell where exactly the wound was because there was so much blood. My glare went from his torso to his face. Buddha looked pale.

"Bruh what the fuck happened?" I bark.

"Momma let Casey hold the towel I'm okay. Go ahead. I'm going to be alright Momma, but right now I need to talk to Casey."

His mother's tears streamed faster down her face as she raised from the couch without a word. She didn't believe he would be okay any more than I did. I sat in her place and held the towel while she leaves the room.

Buddha put his hand on mine and it felt as if he had been playing in the snow. I look up to his eyes.

As the tears that begin to fill his eyes overflowed, rolled down his cheeks only to get lost in his beard, with labored breathing he begin to speak, *"I've loved you like a brother. I need you to watch out for my momma and my sisters. Nobody will do it like you, bruh. I know I can count on you for this. Tell me I can count on you for this.*

"You know you can count on me brother." I assure him."

"I'm glad you and Meredith found your way back to each other."

"Bruh what happened?" I say as my tears began to well up in my eyes.

"My phone is in my back pocket. I got a new supplier that Hitch put me on to, his name is Bristol. I knew I should have checked this cat out more but I was drying up all over after Hitch left." Buddha starts gasping for air.

"Okay bruh, I got you. Just hang tight." I say to Buddha as I turn to one of the other guys in the room and yell *"Call 911 for an ambulance!"*

When I turn back to Buddha, his head is leaned over to the side and his chest is no longer moving in the stuttered motion it had been before. I pull the towel away and see the wound to his chest. I just pull his body to me until I hear a scream from behind me. His mother held up by Callie is in the doorway. It is obvious even from across the room that Buddha is gone. I take the cell phone from Buddha's back pocket and allow his Mother to take him into her arms.

"I'm sorry Casey. He tried to call you earlier before he went to meet this dude. Something about the whole thing wasn't right but our supply needed a re-up and almost everybody is dry. When it all went down he wouldn't let us take him to the hospital." reports Marcus.

I didn't answer him. Instead, I walk out the door leaving it open as I pick up my phone to call Meredith. This will be the second time I call to tell her someone she cares about has been killed but this time will be much worse than the last. My knees buckle when I hear her cheery voice so I brace my body against my car. Just as I begin to speak, the ambulance siren becomes audible. It comes speeding around the corner and stops in front of the house. I point toward the open front door and the paramedics rush inside carrying lifesaving instruments that it will be too late to use.

Hearing Meredith's voice yelling into the phone I remember I had her on the line and put the phone back to my ear.

"What the hell is going on Casey?"

"Baby, you have to come home. We just lost Buddha."

All I hear are screams and the phone drops. I call her back but she doesn't answer. As I go to redial, two police cars pull up. A gunshot wound and nobody talking about how it happened will bring them every time. My brothers in blue approach the house but stop when they reach where I am in the driveway.

"Are you okay? What happened here?" the first officer asks as he sends the other officer into the house gun drawn.

"The suspect isn't on the premise. I arrived to the victim already shot and bleeding out. Call for a sergeant and a homicide detective, I will have to give a statement."

In less than 30 minutes, the Spot is a spectacle of police and yellow tape. I give my story to a sergeant, a lieutenant and two homicide detectives. After a few hours, I am allowed to leave. Buddha's body has been taken by the coroner, Buddha's mother and sisters are taken away by other family members and Marcus will be left to lock up after the other officers leave. There is no reason for me to stay, besides I need to shower and change before I have to pick Meredith up from the airport. Her cousin in Jersey called with her arriving flight information. She assured me that Meredith had calmed down some and will be okay to travel.

I undress to get in the shower. From my front shirt pocket, I pull Buddha's cell phone out. I had forgotten about it and did not mention it in any of the accounts I gave of what happened. I swipe my index finger across the home screen on the front of the phone to reveal a picture of he and Meredith as his background. I quickly touch the phone log icon. There among the list of calls is the name Bristol. I write the phone number down. Before powering the phone off, I also make a note of Hitch's new number. I take the battery out of the phone then throw it and the phone in the trash. All I need is for detectives to trace that phone back to me somehow.

As Meredith appears from the corridor that led from the airline arrival gates, I walk toward her and she just collapses into my arms. I could tell by her face the tears never stopped for long before starting up again the entire time between my bad news and now. I put her in the car and wait on her luggage at the baggage claim. We don't utter a word on the way to my apartment and she doesn't stop crying.

I carry her up the stairs and tuck her in the bed. After she falls asleep from mere exhaustion, I move my arm from around her and get up out the bed. I didn't have a lot of time to prepare for her arrival before having to go pick her up. The last thing I need is for her to see my bloody clothes or Buddha's cell phone. I push the phone deeper into my trash and put the bloody clothes in a plastic bag. I tie the plastic bag and push it down into the trash in the kitchen. My mind is too wide open to go to sleep. Rather than bother Meredith with my tossing and turning, I stay in the living room. I let HBO watch me struggle to come up with a plan.

After finally falling asleep, I opened my eyes to Meredith on her knees beside the couch with her back to me.

"*Baby, you okay?*" I ask a stupid question.

She turns to look at me and nods no. I scoop her up and take her back to the bed. I get in beside her and just hold her as she begins to cry again.

"I can't believe he is gone Casey. What am I supposed to do without my brother? What is Momma, Callie and Cayla supposed to do now?" she sobs.

"I can't believe it either baby but I promise you can count on me. All of you can count on me."

This time it would not be a lie, she can count on me. However she needs me and whatever she needs, I will come through for her. I will come through for Buddha and his family. I did not have a complete plan but I know I have to find Bristol. With a 404 area code, it will not be easy. First I will have to get with Marcus to learn how contact was made and how plans to meet went down. I need all the information he has on this Bristol and the events leading up to Buddha getting shot.

After getting Meredith to eat, I took her to where Callie and the rest of the family were gathered making funeral arrangements for Buddha. Afterwards I go to the administration building to talk to homicide detectives and see where they are with the case. With no witness statements pointing to what happened before Buddha arrived at his mother's house, they are farther behind than the information I have. I call Marcus and arrange for a meeting.

Marcus confirms that Bristol is out of Georgia. He says Buddha had expanded his operation from Birmingham up to Huntsville and down to

Montgomery. He had hopes to spread east into Georgia so when a Georgia contact came up as a possible supplier, he went for it. Buddha didn't have the patience for the normal checking up done on new suppliers, his increased territory needed product and fast. Because Hitch recommended this dude, Buddha arranged a buy with Bristol. The first transaction was small as a test, only enough to fill the Huntsville territory. It went well and so this next buy was bigger and supposed to re-up Birmingham and Montgomery. Marcus tells me that before the money could be exchanged for the product, Bristol shot Buddha after unfriendly words were passed and took the decoy briefcase Buddha was holding. Marcus says he couldn't hear the words spoken because he was back in the car with the briefcase with the money in it waiting for Buddha to call him forward. After Bristol shot, Marcus says he started shooting. As Bristol backed away with the decoy briefcase in one hand he continued shooting at Marcus with the other hand starting a cross fire above Buddha. Marcus says he then drove up to give Buddha cover. Buddha managed to get up into the car and that is when Marcus says he drove off toward the closest hospital. Buddha forcefully redirected him to the Spot where he then called me.

What the hell could have been said for Bristol to have shot Buddha and how does Hitch fit into all of this? I ask Marcus about Hitch and why he left to see what he knows.

"After Meredith left he was on some crazy shit. All he could talk about was how they were going to be together. He always wanted her. He couldn't wait for y'all to break up again. But when Meredith stopped taking his calls he flipped out. He and Buddha got into it but then everything was cool. Hitch left town but left Buddha with enough supply for a while. When Buddha started to get low, he looked for other suppliers around but nobody had enough for all three territories, everybody around here was just too small time. Buddha called Hitch up but he'd gone back to Cali and the nearest contact he had was in Georgia."

"So Hitch didn't really know this Bristol dude, he had just done business with him before?"

"That's what I got from it. But I don't think Hitch would set Buddha up, they didn't have real beef."

"I appreciate the info Marcus."

"If there is anything I can do, just let me know. Buddha was like family to me too."

Marcus may not think Hitch had anything to do with it but I wasn't so sure. That dude always did rub me the wrong way even before I realized he wanted Meredith. I pull out the paper I had written his number on and dial.

"*I'm surprised it took this long for you to call.*" Hitch said.

"*Why didn't you call me?*"

"*We aren't exactly buddies and I don't know how involved you are with this thing.*"

"*What thing?*"

"*Look I did not know Bristol was a psychopath when I hooked him up with Buddha. You know Buddha was my man.*"

"*Where is this Bristol?*"

"*He's back in Georgia. He is not small time, he has a little army over there. He supplies most of the big operations over in G-A. Word is, he knocked off Buddha to start distribution west of his supply operation.*"

"*A big fish in a little pond, huh? Alright.*" I hang up. No need in a good-bye, I still don't like his ass.

If this cat wants to get started in distribution, then he'll be expecting Marcus to take over Buddha's three territories. If I can make it look like they split back off after Buddha's death, then Bristol might take the bait to make a run for the territories one by one. I will need to get Marcus on board to make it look good then create some buzz around the separation of territories. I can get Battlekat in

Montgomery to try and set up a meet with Bristol for supplies, giving the impression of a rogue lieutenant making a move to take over his area.

It didn't take long for Bristol to take the bait. He is on the way to the Laicos Club, the most prominent strip club in Montgomery. If this meet and greet went well, then the buy will go down at the nearby Capitol Inn on Goldthwaite Street. When I arrive, I get a seat in the back corner away from the table Battlekat chose for the meeting. Soon after a dude in a linen suit followed by two other guys dress in jeans and oversized shirts enter the club. After looking around a bit, they are directed to Battlekat's table by a waitress. I watch as Battlekat gives the two dudes that came with Bristol money to tip at the main stage. He and Bristol talk and drink from the Ciroc bottle buried in ice. After about 45 minutes, I see Battlekat call for the waitress I know the meeting is over and it is time for the buy. I get up and leave out the door. The plan is for Battlekat to get them to follow him down North Holt and cross over Clay Street to get to Goldthwaite. Meanwhile I am taking the shorter route of Mobile Street to Goldthwaite so I will arrive at the Capitol Inn first. I see them pull up a few minutes later. I watch Battlekat and his two guards walk in front of Bristol and his two guys. I am sure Bristol is thinking he is in charge of the situation all the way up until all the doors of the bottom floor hotel rooms open at once to reveal a row of men with guns pointed right at Bristol and his two flunkies. Battlekat and his two guards turn around. Battlekat picks up his phone and mine rings.

As I walk slowly toward Bristol. The two guards are picked off by two different shooters from each end of the hotel. Bristol drops to his knees. He must be trying to make a deal, as I walk up I hear Battlekat say, "*That's not up to me. You see my man here got a few words he needs to have with you.*"

As Bristol turns to look at me, he asks "*Who are you?*"

I feel the air stop flowing to my lungs as heavily. My heart beats so hard it seems to be beating like a bass drum.

"*I'm the one that has to console my girlfriend because you shot her brother, you sonofabitch.*"

POW

The shot rings out and Bristols body falls.

"*Damn, you got him right in the head man. That police training ain't nothing nice.*" Battlekat brags. "*We're on clean up duty, you go ahead.*"

As I walk back to my car I feel nothing. As I drive back to Birmingham, my hands don't shake and I don't feel sorry. If I am honest with myself, I would say it feels good.

Buddha's funeral was abuzz of revenge having been taken. It didn't stop Buddha's mother's tears, nor his sisters' tears, nor Meredith's tears. It wouldn't stop mine either, if I could conjure them.

****

"*Welcome to Major Fraud Detective Canyon. Is that your lovely wife in the picture there on your desk?*"

"*Thank you and yes it is.*"

As I look up to see who I'm addressing, I see Hitch. He's in plain clothes with a badge on one side of his belt and on the other side next to his holstered gun an ID that says: Chris Hitchens, Narcotics Department.

Book 2: Canyon Deep

Now Detective Canyon, Casey is settling into married life with Meredith when the past and a promise sucks him back into a world he thought he'd left behind. After getting fatally shot and falling into a coma, will Hitchens be able to tie Casey to Bristol's murder? Or will Casey's mystery ally be able to cover all his tracks in time?

Are you ready for book 2 in the Canyon Series? Join our mailing list to be informed of its and other publications by S.W. Cannon including book 3, Canyon Echo.
(http://www.authorswcannon.com/apps/auth/signup)

Let's talk about the book and the characters.
http://www.authorswcannon.com/apps/forums/

Book Clubs, check this out:
http://www.authorswcannon.com/book-clubs

About the Author

S. W. Cannon was raised in and still lives in Birmingham, Alabama. She was excited to include the area as a minor character in her first book. She has had a love of writing for years and getting her feet wet with blogs and a local magazine was just the beginning. While attending Author Curtis Bunn's National Book Club Conference, (http://www.nationalbookclubconference.com) she was inspired by the authors in attendance to begin her first book. Keeping in touch with Author Rickey Teems, II for advice on writing, book tours, etc... was just the encouragement she needed to drive her talent. Meeting Author Robb Lee and reading his book *Insignificant Others* is what motivated her to make her first book a novella. By far, the most inspiration and encouragement came from Christopher Cannon. There are few people in life that have supported her as much as he.

www.AuthorSWCannon.com

58721387R00063

Made in the USA
Charleston, SC
17 July 2016